The

LIGHTHOUSE FAMILY

THE EAGLE

Other books in the
Lighthouse Family series

The Storm

The Whale

The Turtle

The Octopus

The Otter

The Sea Lion

The
LIGHTHOUSE FAMILY

THE EAGLE

BY CYNTHIA RYLANT
ILLUSTRATED BY PRESTON McDANIELS

BEACH LANE BOOKS
New York   London   Toronto   Sydney   New Delhi

BEACH LANE BOOKS

An imprint of Simon & Schuster Children's Publishing Division
1230 Avenue of the Americas, New York, New York 10020

The text for this book is set in Centaur.
The illustrations for this book are rendered in graphite.
Manufactured in China
0618 SCP
4 6 8 10 9 7 5

Library of Congress Cataloging-in-Publication Data
Rylant, Cynthia.
The lighthouse family. The eagle / Cynthia Rylant; illustrated by Preston McDaniels.—
1st ed.
p. cm.
Summary: Two mice that live in a lighthouse along with a dog, a cat, and another
mouse, lose their compass while exploring the forest, and learn to use their instincts
before being rescued by an eagle.
ISBN 978-0-689-86243-4
[1. Lighthouses—Fiction. 2. Mice—Fiction. 3. Cats—Fiction. 4. Dogs—Fiction.
5. Eagles—Fiction.] I. Title: Eagle. II. McDaniels, Preston, ill. III. Title.
PZ7.R982 Lg 2004
[Fic]—dc22   2003018636
ISBN 978-1-4442-9936-2 (eBook)

For our beautiful daughters, Abby and Elizabeth
—P. McD.

Contents

1. *Fall* 8

2. *A Way* 16

3. *The Forest* 24

4. *Which Way?* 34

5. *Stanley* 42

6. *The Stars* 50

1. *Fall*

On a cliff far above the blue waters of the ocean there stood a solitary lighthouse, and in this lighthouse lived a family.

They were: Pandora, the cat; Seabold, the dog; and Whistler, Lila, and Tiny, three mouse children.

This family had not always been together. They once were scattered far and wide, and none had ever guessed they would find one another one day.

For many years Pandora had lived all alone at the lighthouse, bearing her loneliness so she might save others by keeping the light burning.

Seabold had been a sailor, steering his little boat *Adventure* across the waters of the world.

And the three children—Whistler, Lila, and

Tiny—had lived within the walls of an orphanage, until the night they escaped to the sea.

But one day Seabold washed ashore in a storm and Pandora found him. Then Pandora and Seabold, in turn, found the children, lost and adrift in the ocean.

Thus these wanderers came together, made a home, and thereafter they were the lighthouse family.

Now it was fall. The children and Pandora and Seabold had enjoyed a lovely summer. Through the long days the children had collected rose petals and lavender, and now Pandora was kept busy each morning in the kitchen,

making rose petal and lavender jellies for the winter table.

Outside on these crisp, blue days, Seabold—with Tiny tucked snug in the roll of his wool cap—tended the fall garden. He planted onions, covered the beans, harvested the carrots and potatoes for cold storage, and sowed peas. Tiny watched his every move, full of delight. Tiny was very attached to Seabold.

And on these splendid mornings Whistler and Lila, the oldest children, explored the rocky shore. At low tide they climbed over the slippery stones, careful not to step on the barnacles or disturb the small crabs living in the crevices. If one of them disturbed a sea squirt who was hiding, the mice got a surprise shower!

Sometimes a bald eagle left his nest at the top of a fir tree in the woods beyond the shore and soared grandly above the children. Whistler and Lila arched back their heads and watched him glide.

"What do you think his name is?" Whistler asked Lila this morning.

"Something impressive, I expect," Lila said. "Like him."

"Perhaps 'Higginbotham'," said Whistler.

"'Higginbotham'?" asked Lila. "What sort of name is that?"

"I saw it in a book once," said Whistler. "It seems an important name."

Lila watched as the eagle flew farther and farther, disappearing into the clouds.

"Maybe so," she said. "Maybe that's Higginbotham."

Whistler looked toward the thick, tall trees from which the eagle had flown. He sighed.

"I wish Pandora would allow us to explore the woods," he said.

"She's afraid we might become lost," said Lila, picking up a sea lettuce to take home.

Whistler and Lila looked silently across the shore toward the dark forest.

"I suppose we might get lost," said Whistler.

"Yes," said Lila. "We might."

They stood gazing at the deep, green woods. Both wanted very much to go there.

2. *A Way*

With the fall, lighthouse keeping had again become serious work for Pandora and Seabold. The few summer months of fair weather had allowed them some rest from their duties. But now the rains were coming back, fog season had begun, and there was always the chance of a storm.

Thus Seabold rose up from his bed several times during the night to check the light and make sure the flame still burned and the glass remained clear. Pandora wound the mechanism that rotated the giant lens each morning and night so that the light beamed out its constant signal: two seconds on, six seconds eclipse. It had never failed. But Seabold worried about the flame.

So he tended the lamp through the night. Then, just before daybreak, he snuffed out the flame, closed the curtains, and joined the family for breakfast.

Mornings were chilly enough now for a fire, and the deep warmth of the kitchen stove made everyone happy. They all sat together at Pandora's table for a porridge of hickory nuts, cherries, and warm maple syrup.

Seabold scooped up Tiny and put her in his eggcup, as always. It was Tiny's favorite place at the table.

"Seabold, may we go into the forest?" asked Whistler.

Lila looked at Whistler in surprise. She hadn't known he was going to ask this. At least not so directly!

Seabold looked toward Pandora and smiled.

"Pandora worries you will become lost," said Seabold. "And so do I."

Pandora gravely nodded her head.

"Well then," Whistler began, "how does someone make sure he doesn't get lost? How did you sail the ocean without becoming lost?"

Seabold offered Tiny a small spoonful of porridge.

"I had a binnacle," said Seabold.

"What is a binnacle?" asked Lila.

"A binnacle points a sailor in the right direction," said Seabold. "On water, one uses a binnacle. On land, one uses a compass."

Whistler looked at Lila. Lila looked at Pandora.

"Pandora, may we learn to use a compass?" asked Lila.

And that was how the children found a way to the forest.

3. The Forest

The day that Whistler and Lila prepared for their journey into the trees was a beautiful one. The bluffs above the waves were covered with what Pandora called "paintbrush"—hundreds of wildflowers in reds, oranges, and pinks. The sky was sapphire blue. The soft winds were cool and clean.

Pandora helped Lila with her sweater and bonnet while Seabold stood nearby and reminded Whistler of all the rules:

"Watch the compass.

"Never separate.

"And come home when the sun is directly overhead. It will be time for lunch and Pandora is baking tarts."

"Tarts!" said Whistler. "We shall *sniff* our way back home!"

"Sniff and watch the compass," said Seabold.

Lila looked at Seabold as she straightened her bonnet.

"We will be very careful, Seabold," she said. "We are very good with the compass now."

"That you are," said Seabold. "I do believe you could find your way to the North Pole from here."

"I have a few friends there you might visit," Pandora said with a smile. "Among them a walrus who sings."

"Really?" asked Whistler.

"How did you meet a walrus?" asked Lila.

"Oh, he was just passing through," said Pandora. "And he had a sore throat."

"Did you help him?" asked Lila.

"A cup of roseroot tea and he was singing like a bell," said Pandora.

"Well, we aren't going as far as the North Pole," said Whistler. "At least not today."

Pandora smiled again.

"I should hope not," she said. "One should always come home for tarts."

"Yes," said Lila.

Seabold handed the children their twine bags and a walnut flask filled with water.

"The compass," reminded Seabold.

"Right-o," said Whistler.

And with a kiss from each on Tiny's soft head, the two children stepped out the door.

"I think that once we are in the forest, we should search for a fairy ring," Lila said to Whistler as they walked along the cliff toward the woods.

"What is a fairy ring?" asked Whistler.

"It's a circle of mushrooms under a tree," said Lila. "Once, Pandora told me that when she was little, she collected them for her mother. Her mother cooked them into a nice soup."

"I'm just hoping to look at bugs," said Whistler.

"Ugh," said Lila.

As the children drew nearer to the dark forest, the trees seemed to grow taller and taller with each step. Hemlock, cedar, spruce, and fir—all rose up to the sky in tight rank, blocking out the sunlight.

Whistler checked the compass as he and Lila looked behind them toward home.

"I know where we are," said Whistler.

"So do I," said Lila. "I can see the lighthouse right over there."

"Well," said Whistler, "in a fog the compass would have guided us."

"I am counting on it," said Lila, "for I can already taste those tarts."

Looking back toward home one last time, the two children turned and walked into the woods.

"It's so chilly in here," Lila said, "but I like it."

Whistler looked up at the branches hung with lichens like long, gray beards.

"The trees feel old," he said.

"And wise," answered Lila.

The children walked farther. Everywhere giant ferns and mossy logs covered the forest floor. Whistler stepped inside one of the logs.

"There's a good, green smell in here," he said.

Lila stepped in too.

"This would be perfect for playing house," she said.

"Even pirates," said Whistler. "It feels like a ship."

The children walked even farther. The forest was so quiet. It was different from the seashore, which was always noisy with the beating of waves

and the calling of gulls. The forest was still. It seemed to be listening to the soft voices of two little mice carrying a walnut flask and a compass.

"Look!" said Lila. "A fairy ring!"

Indeed, at the foot of a tall fir, in a bed of green moss, lay a circle of soft, heavy mushrooms.

"They're beautiful," said Lila.

"I know," said Whistler.

The fairy ring glistened in the cool, damp moss.

"I almost don't want to pick them," said Lila.

"Neither do I," said Whistler. "They're perfect."

"Let's leave them," Lila said. "We'll bring home huckleberries instead."

"Right," answered Whistler. "We'll check the compass now and start turning back."

He reached into a pocket. Then he reached into another pocket. He went back to the first pocket. Then he went back to the second.

"Lila . . . ," Whistler began.

His sister looked at him.

"Oh no," she said.

4. *Which Way?*

"I'm sure we'll find our way back," said Whistler as they walked in the direction he thought would take them home.

"After all, we've hardly traveled far," he added.

"I have a feeling we'll miss the tarts," said Lila.

"How could I have lost the compass?" asked Whistler. "How?"

"It's easy to lose things," said Lila. "I do it all the time."

Whistler stopped. He listened to the forest a moment.

"What is it?" asked Lila. "Should we turn the other way?"

"No," said Whistler, "I don't think so. I believe

this is the right way. I just feel it somehow.

"Anyway," he continued, "Seabold will be so disappointed in me."

"Seabold is never disappointed in us," said Lila.

It was true. Seabold understood mistakes.

"Well, I do wish I hadn't lost his compass," said Whistler.

Whistler stopped again.

"Wait," he said.

"What?" asked Lila. She stopped too.

"Just wait," said Whistler. He listened.

"Is someone coming to help us?" asked Lila.

"Shhh," said Whistler.

The two mice remained very still and quiet.

"It's the surf!" cried Whistler. "We're near the surf!"

The children hurried through the forest, following the faint sounds of the ocean's ebb and flow.

"We're getting closer," said Lila. "I hear gulls."

"Yes!" said Whistler. "Hurry!"

Ahead the children saw a light glowing against the forest's edge. They saw a blue horizon. And they ran as fast as they could, away from the thick darkness of trees.

"We're out!" said Whistler, stepping out onto a rocky bluff.

"Hooray!" said Lila. The ocean was blue and beautiful below them.

"But which way is the lighthouse?" asked Lila. She looked far down the shore in one direction,

then far down the shore in another. There was no lighthouse.

"Which way do we go?" she asked.

"Perhaps I can help," said a voice behind them.

The children turned around.

It was Higginbotham. And he had the compass.

5. Stanley

"I saw it fall out of your pocket," said the eagle, handing the compass to Whistler.

"Amazing!" said Whistler. "Thank you!"

"I see everything," said the eagle.

"I'm sure you do," said Lila. "My name is Lila, and this is my brother, Whistler."

"Pleased to meet you," said the eagle. "I'm Stanley."

"Stanley?" asked Whistler.

"Are you sure?" asked Lila.

The eagle peered down his beak.

"I have been Stanley all my life," he said.

"We thought you were Higginbotham," said Lila. She explained why.

"Oh," said the eagle. "Well, it's a fine name. It's just not mine."

"That's all right," said Whistler. "Stanley is friendlier."

"Why did you not return the compass until now?" asked Lila.

"I wanted to give you a chance to help yourselves," said Stanley. "You did a fine job."

"Thank you!" Whistler said proudly. He was glad Stanley had given them that chance.

"Instinct is everything," said Stanley.

"Exactly," said Whistler.

"But your instinct isn't telling you which way to go now, I see," said Stanley.

"My instinct is telling me only that I'm hungry," said Lila.

"Yes," said Stanley. "Come along then."

"Where are we going?" asked Whistler.

"To my home," said the eagle. And in an instant he scooped up both children, placed them in his

vest pocket, and flew them to the top of the tallest tree in the forest.

"Astounding!" cried Whistler from Stanley's nest.

"Astonishing!" said Lila.

Neither of the mice had ever climbed a tree. And here they were, in the tallest tree of all, looking out across the sharp peaks of firs and cedars that stretched away from them as far as they could see.

"I didn't know a forest stretches so far," said Whistler.

"It stretches forever," said Lila, "like the ocean."

Whistler and Lila looked at each other.

"We might have become lost," said Lila.

"We might have," said Whistler.

"But you didn't," said Stanley.

"Thank you for watching over us," Whistler said to Stanley.

"Yes, thank you," said Lila.

"No trouble at all," said Stanley. "Let me fix you a plate of pine nuts."

"Wonderful," said Lila.

"Do you like tarts, Stanley?" asked Whistler.

"Oh yes," said the eagle. "Passionately."

Whistler smiled.

"Then with my compass," he said, "we shall soon find you some."

6. The Stars

The eagle walked the children home.

"It's good of you to walk to the lighthouse with us, Stanley," said Whistler. "We know you could get there so much faster on your own."

"Well, I wanted to see you put the compass to good use," said Stanley, "which you surely have," he added, pointing ahead.

"The lighthouse!" cried Lila. "Home!"

"What is that *delicious* smell?" asked Stanley.

"I told you," Whistler said with a grin.

Right on time for tarts, the mice walked up the path to the lighthouse with the tall, imposing eagle in tow. Looking out the kitchen door, Seabold said to Pandora, "I think the children have had an adventure."

The lunch of plum and thorn apple tarts was a wonderful affair. Seabold and Stanley had much to talk about, both being old travelers of the sea. And of course, the children had to describe their journey into the woods.

"I am glad you left the fairy ring behind," said Pandora. "I believe it brought you luck. You did find your way out of the woods without a compass."

"Yes," said Lila, "it must have been the fairy ring."

"I think it was my nose," said Whistler.

"Your nose?" asked Pandora.

"I think I sniffed us in the right direction," said Whistler.

"Oh yes," said Seabold. "I did that all the time when I was sailing."

"I thought you used a binnacle," said Lila.

"The binnacle just confirmed my instincts," answered Seabold. "Instinct is everything."

"Oh yes," said Stanley, nodding his regal head before biting into another tart.

In the course of lunchtime conversation, the family found out that Stanley was also an amateur astronomer. As he spoke of this, he pulled a worn book from his pocket.

"This is my Starry Sky Notebook," said Stanley. "In it I keep all my observations."

"Amazing!" said Whistler. "May we see?"

The eagle spread open the pages of his notebook and with the children standing on his shoulders and Tiny clinging to the top of his head, Stanley showed them his drawings of the stars.

"Here is the constellation Little Dog," said Stanley. "And here is the Dog Star."

"More dogs in the heavens than I ever knew," said Seabold.

"And here is my favorite constellation," said Stanley with a smile. "The Eagle."

"It does look like an eagle!" said Lila.

"Perhaps," Pandora said to Stanley, "you might like to stargaze from the catwalk of our lighthouse."

"Oh yes!" said Whistler. "You could show us all the constellations!"

"Please, could you?" asked Lila.

And so that evening on the catwalk of their lighthouse, the family assembled with the eagle who would show them the stars. Whistler had made his own Starry Sky Notebook and as Stanley spoke, Whistler took notes. Stanley pointed out the Dippers and the great Bull and the Seven Sisters. He showed the family how the moon follows a path across the night sky.

"I have followed the moon many a time," said Seabold. In his voice was the pride of a sailor who had traveled well.

When the gazing was done, Pandora made tea for everyone, then the eagle set about to return home.

"Don't forget to watch for shooting stars," he reminded the children. "And make a wish on every one."

"Thank you, Stanley," said Seabold. "Thank you for everything."

When the eagle was gone, Whistler and Lila returned to the catwalk to watch the sky for another hour.

In that hour they saw sixteen shooting stars, and they each made sixteen perfect wishes.